For Cora and Neil,
with love from
Aunt Cait

HYLAS

Hylas Publishing

First Published in 2005 by Hylas Publishing
129 Main Street, Irvington, New York, 10533

Publisher: Sean Moore
Creative Director: Karen Prince
Book Design: Miles Parsons and Pat Covert
Produced by: Cliff Road Books

First American Edition published in 2005
02 03 04 05 10 9 8 7 6 5 4 3 2 1

ISBN: 1-59258-100-5

Photography by Keith Harrelson
Costumes by Janet Tatum
Flowers by Dorothy McDaniel's Flower Market

Grateful acknowledgment is made to Margaret Jones Davis and staff at
Creative Dog Training in Birmingham, Alabama, without whom this
book would not have been possible, and especially to (in order of
appearance): Lily Sizemore, Rusty Davis, Allie-Oop Buford, Louie
Barnett, Anna Brockway, Mighty Quinn Buford, Tucker Moffett,
Bertrand, and Heather Barnett.

Printed and bound in Italy
Distributed by National Book Network

www.hylaspublishing.com

CINDERELLA

HYLAS

Once upon a time there lived a young girl
named Cinderella. She was kind and pure.

Cinderella lived with her wicked stepmother and two wicked stepsisters. They were jealous of her kind nature and were cruel to her.

*O*ne day in the mail, the family got an invitation to the Prince's ball.

Cinderella wanted to go! When her
stepsisters saw her excitement, they laughed.
They knew she would not fit in.

Cinderella helped her stepsisters and stepmother get ready for the ball. She finished her chores just as her stepsisters were leaving. "What will you wear to the ball, Cinderella?" her stepsisters teased. They knew she only had rags to wear.

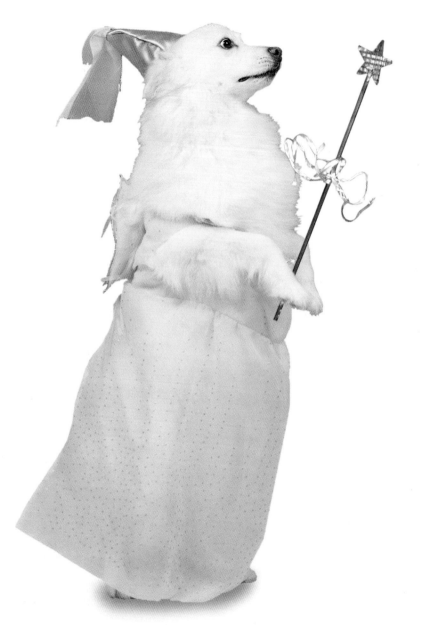

When Cinderella was alone, she sat by the fire and cried. Suddenly there was a gentle tap at the door. Cinderella opened the door and saw the most beautiful creature.

"My child," said the vision, "Do not be sad. I am your fairy godmother. I am here to grant your wish. We must get you ready for the Prince's ball!"

"Now, bring me a pumpkin." Cinderella did as she was told. The fairy godmother waved her wand and in an instant the pumpkin changed into a beautiful carriage.

"Now bring me six white mice." Cinderella gathered
the mice. The fairy godmother waved her wand and
the mice changed into six strong horses.

"Oh fairy godmother!" said Cinderella. "I am so happy! But what shall I wear? I have no gown." "My child, do not worry." With a wave of her wand, Cinderella's rags changed into the most beautiful gown in the world. At her feet were sparkling glass slippers.

$\mathcal{C}$inderella climbed into her carriage. As she rode away, her fairy godmother said, "You must return by midnight, Cinderella. At midnight everything will change back to what it was. Your gown will be rags. Your carriage will be a pumpkin. Your horses will be mice!"

Cinderella promised to be home before midnight. She rode to the ball with wonder in her eyes.

When Cinderella arrived at the ball, the Prince greeted her kindly. He had never seen anyone so beautiful. In fact, no one at the ball had ever seen anyone quite like Cinderella.

They all wondered who she was.
Even her stepsisters did not
recognize this exotic princess.

$\mathcal{C}$inderella danced with the Prince. They hardly spoke a word. Suddenly, Cinderella heard the clock chime. "Oh no!" she thought, "The clock is striking midnight!"

She dashed out of the ball and raced down the palace steps. Along the way she lost one of her glass slippers.

The next day the Prince sent a messenger with the glass slipper to every house. Every lady in the land must try it on. When the Prince found the Princess who fit into that slipper, he would marry her.

The ladies all tried hard to squeeze into the slipper. Even Cinderella's wicked stepsisters!

Cinderella was last to try on the slipper. Her stepsisters laughed. "It will never fit her! She is no princess!" But it was a perfect fit.

Cinderella smiled and pulled from
her pocket the matching glass slipper.

$\mathcal{S}$uddenly the fairy godmother appeared. She waved her wand and Cinderella's rags changed into a beautiful gown. Her stepsisters were ashamed. They begged Cinderella to forgive them. Cinderella did. Then she married the Prince, and they frolicked happily ever after.

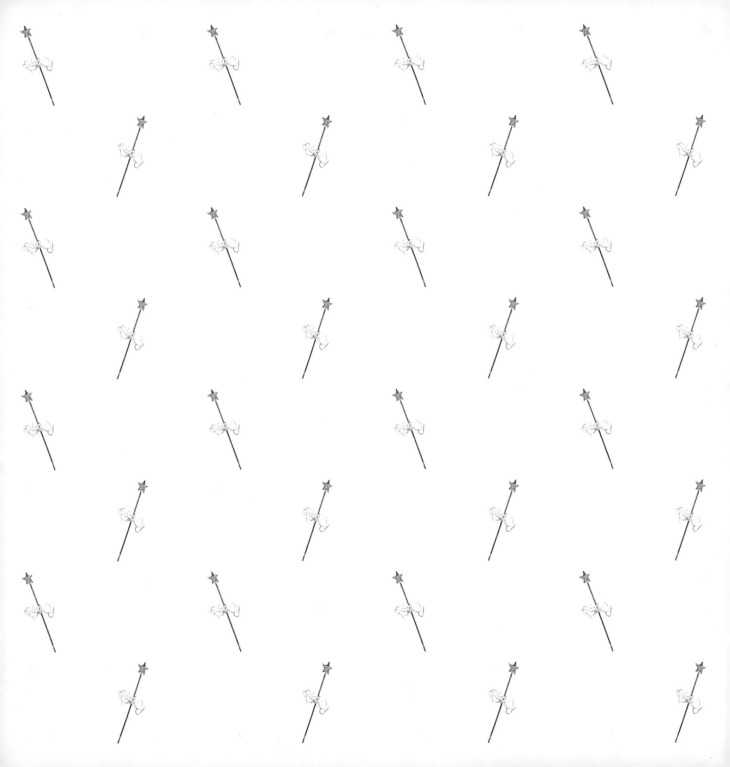